These 30 stories were made up as bedtime tales for my beautiful granddaughter, Elyssa.

She lives far away in London and making up these stories helps to make the distance seem less.

Her cousin, Yannou, also likes to hear of the magical adventures Martha has with her friend, Mary.

Some of these stories contain characters from my other book of bedtime stories: *'The Rabbit with Three Ears'*

GJ Abercrombie

Edinburgh

2019

SWEET DREAMS

GJ abmb

For Elyssa and Yannou

Chapter 1

Meet Martha

Martha the Magical Mouse lives in Camberwell, London, England.

If you looked at her you would not notice that she is magical; she is quite an ordinary-looking mouse. She has a small, brown body, a pointy, pink nose with short, black whiskers. She has large, round ears which make her very good at hearing, just like her distant cousin Trevor. I call him a 'distant' cousin because he lives far, far away in Portobello, Edinburgh, Scotland (... and he's a rabbit!).

Martha's favourite colour is yellow and most days she wears a yellow ribbon tied in a bow around her neck.

When Martha was very young, she discovered that she could do magic things, sometimes .... Let me explain how she found out .....

One day, Martha had gone into her local library in Camberwell. She was looking for a recipe for a nice chocolate cake for her friend's birthday. She saw a cake book with a photograph of a lady on the front of it.

More
Yummy
Cakes

"That lady looks like my Granny, Lucy Mouse", she thought. When she opened the book, she got a surprise. Written inside were the words:

Use the Library Link, Martha!

At first Martha did not know what this meant but she looked around the library and saw a door with 'Library Link' written on it. She went through the door and suddenly she was in a completely different library.

A sign on the wall said:

'Welcome to Corstorphine Library, Edinburgh'.

"That's where my Granny works", thought Martha. Then she heard someone say "Hello Poppet". (Martha's Granny always calls her Poppet). "Hi Granny", she said and gave her a big squeezy hug. Martha's Granny, Lucy Mouse, told her she had special news for her.

"I want to tell you that all the mice in our family are magical! *(All the rabbits in the family have three ears, but that's another story.)* I can tell you a little bit about the magic but mostly you'll need to find out for yourself", she said to an amazed Martha.

"If you twitch your nose very quickly, your whiskers will turn gold and start to shine a little. When this happens you'll feel all tingly and magical and that's when you'll be able to say magic spells", Granny Lucy explained.

"I can't tell you any more, Tootie-Pie",

(Martha's Granny always calls her Tootie-Pie.)

"But you should try to keep your magic a secret. You can tell your close friends but it would be best not to let EVERYONE know about it. Go back through the Library Link now; and good luck my Little Sweetheart"

(Martha's Granny always calls her 'Little Sweetheart')

(She calls Martha lots of different things, doesn't she?)

When Martha got back home, she found that she really could make things happen when she felt magical. All she had to do was say a spell out loud.

One day she noticed a little rip in the material of her yellow ribbon. She wondered if she could make a magic spell to fix it. She twitched her nose to make herself magical and then she tried a spell.

She said:

"Mend my ribbon!"

Suddenly, a needle with yellow thread appeared and sewed up the small tear on her yellow bow.

"Well, that was amazing!" she thought,

"I'll try another spell".

She decided she was thirsty and would like a drink.

She shouted:

"Make me a cup of tea!"

… and the kettle flew over to the sink, filled itself with water and then switched itself on!

"WOW!" she cried, "this is great fun. I can get all my housework jobs done like this. I'll never have to work hard again".

Next, she tried:

"Wash my dishes!"

… but nothing happened!

Martha was puzzled. She could not understand why the first two spells worked but the third one did not. By this time her whiskers had stopped glowing and she did not feel magical anymore.

She drank her 'magic-made' cup of tea and admired her 'magic-mended' ribbon while she tried to work it all out.

Later on, she had to wash the dishes by herself because her 'Wash My Dishes' spell still did not work. Her plate was very messy because she had eaten beans for her tea!

She was still puzzled by this mystery when she went to bed that night.

"I wonder why some of my magic spells work and others don't", she thought as she fell asleep in her cosy bed.

Martha dreamt about everything that had happened:

- The Library Link visit to Granny Lucy
- The magic sewing
- The kettle filling itself
- The spell that did not work

Chapter 2

Spelling Lesson

The next day Martha thought she would try again. She twitched her nose very quickly just like her Granny had told her and soon her whiskers glowed. She felt magical again so she tried a few new spells:

"Open the door!"

... nothing happened.

"Make my bed!"

... the pillows and quilt flew up from the floor and landed tidily on the bed!

"Well, that one worked", thought Martha.

"Tidy the kitchen!"

... again nothing happened.

"Move my coat into the cupboard!"

... her coat flew up off of the back of the kitchen chair and into the cupboard in the hall (where it should have been in the first place).

"Hhhmmmm", thought Martha, "I'm beginning to see a pattern here."

(Can you see the pattern?)

Martha noticed that each time her magic worked the first word of the spell began with the letter 'M'.

She decided to try it out.

She twitched her nose and as soon as her whiskers glowed she said:

"I'd like a slice of toast!"

... and nothing happened.

Then she said:

"<u>May</u> I please have a slice of toast?"

... and the bread-bin opened and a slice of bread jumped right into the toaster by itself!

It worked!

"I'll try another one", she thought.

She made herself magical again and repeated the spell that she had tried the night before:

"Wash My dishes!"

… again, nothing happened.

She then said:

"My dishes are dirty, please wash them!"

… and the plates and cups and bowls all jumped into the basin in the sink which filled itself with warm soapy water. Then the dishes all leapt out of the water onto the drying rack beside the sink. They were all shiny and sparkling clean.

"YES!" cried Martha.

She knew how to do her magic and she was going to have fun experimenting with it!

She thought that her Granny Lucy would be very proud of her!

Chapter 3

Mmmmmm Magic

As well as being magical (from time to time, when her whiskers were golden), Martha loved to do gymnastics (or gym, for short).

She practised her gym almost every day. (She called it 'Grampa Gym' for a joke because her Grampa was called 'Jim')

Martha usually got up early in the morning and started exercising.

She always started with a warm-up of stretching. She stretched her arms and legs out as far as she could.

(Can you do that?)

She was very good at star-jumps.

Star jumps are where you jump up into the air and point your arms and legs out in different directions to make a star.

(Can you do that?)

Most people can make a five-pointed star with their arms and legs and head. With two arms, two legs, one head and one tail Martha could make a six-pointed star!

She could also do head-stands.

Head-stands are where you put your hands and your head on the ground and balance with your feet sticking up in the air.

(Can you do that? It's quite hard.)

Being a mouse, Martha had two big ears on the ground and these helped her to keep steady.

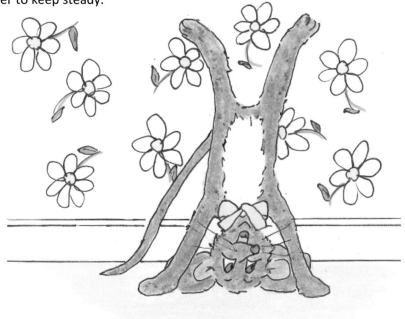

After practising her gymnastics, Martha always felt hungry. What did she fancy to eat?

Now, Martha the Magical Mouse loved biscuits, especially the sweet, spicy ones called 'perkins'.

That day, after her 'gym', she looked in her biscuit tin but she had no perkins left. She could have baked some herself but she decided to try some magic.

(Do you remember how she becomes magical?)

That's right; she twitches her nose until her whiskers turn gold and start to glow. As soon as she felt all tingly and magical, she said:

"Mmmmmm, I'd love some perkins!"

… and a plate with three of her favourite biscuits appeared. She nibbled away at them then, without thinking about it properly, she said:

"Mmmmmm, delicious!

I could eat 100 perkins for my lunch!"

Suddenly it started raining perkins! They landed everywhere: on the kitchen table and chairs and in the kitchen sink. One landed in her goldfish bowl and her pet fish started nibbling at it. Another one fell down the toilet, so she decided not to eat that one!

It took ages to tidy up the mess. Martha ate as many as she could but soon her tummy was full.

She put some into her biscuit tin and wrapped others up to give to her friends.

Some of the perkins had broken when they fell so she put the crumbs on her window-sill for the birds to eat.

So many perkins!

She thought to herself, "I'll need to be careful what I say while I am magical, especially if it begins with the letter 'M'."

"But it's so hard not to say 'Mmmmmm' while eating lovely perkins", she added, licking her lips.

Chapter 4

Upside-Down Magic

(Do you remember that Martha likes doing gymnastics?)

As well as doing star-jumps and head-stands, she also did more energetic exercises. She would run and jump about her house, hanging from the lights and swinging on the door frames.

Sometimes she made so much noise crashing about that her neighbours complained and banged on the walls to make her be quiet.

She also liked going to her local park and playing on all the slides and swings. No-one complained about the noise she made there!

One day, Martha was playing on the climbing frame at the park. She was hanging upside-down by her tail. Suddenly she was very thirsty and decided to 'magic up' a drink of water.

She twitched her nose to become magical and then thought of a spell. (*Remember, all her spells had to begin with the letter 'M'*). Martha was getting quite good at making up spells. She said:

"My mouth is dry. I need some water!"

... but nothing happened!

"That's strange", she thought "it should have worked; the word '<u>My</u>' begins with 'M'".

Then she said:

"Why is my magic not working?

Where is my water?"

Suddenly a big cup of water appeared in her hand but, because she was upside-down, the water poured all over her face!

"AARRGGGH!" she shouted, "I'm soaking wet now".

She climbed down onto the grass and tried to work out what had happened.

She looked around and saw a big supermarket with a large 'M' as its logo. She thought it looked both familiar and strange at the same time.

Suddenly she realised that while she was hanging upside-down it had looked a bit different; it looked like the letter 'W' rather than the letter 'M'. That's because the letter 'W' is like an upside-down 'M'.

Martha wondered if her spells only worked if they begin with the letter 'W' while she is upside-down. She decided to try it out. She sat on the grass and said:

"White chocolate, please!"

... and nothing happened (as she expected).

Then she did a head-stand on the grass and repeated her spell:

"White chocolate, please!"

… and a bar of her favourite treat appeared beside her. She was delighted and ate it all up.

"This magic is quite tricky", she thought as she walked home to get dried. (She was still wet from the water incident.)

When she got home, she made a cup of tea as she was still thirsty. She switched on the kettle herself because she'd had quite enough magic for one day.

Later on, she phoned her Granny in Edinburgh to tell her what she had discovered about her magic.

"I told you that you would need to find out about your magic by yourself. Every mouse's magic works differently but it sounds like you are beginning to understand how yours works. Just keep trying things and use your power with goodness and kindness", she said.

Her Granny also reminded her that she could tell someone about her magic; but only someone she trusted completely.

Martha told her Granny that she had a good friend called Mary and that she had decided to share the secret with her.

"That's nice", said Granny, "but, remember not to use your magic too much. It's unfair to other people if you use it all the time".

Chapter 5

Martha's Friend Mary

Martha's best friend was a little, grey mouse called Mary.

Like Martha, Mary wore a ribbon tied in a bow around her neck; but hers was green.

Green is Mary's favourite colour.

(Do you remember what Martha's favourite colour is? … Yellow)

(What's your favourite colour? Blue, Pink, Red, Brown?)

Mary was the only other person who knew that Martha was magical and she promised she would keep it a secret between the two of them.

Mary wasn't magical, but she was very musical!

She was always singing and dancing and making music. She could play any instrument you can think of: Guitar, piano, drums, flute, cello, tuba, harmonica … anything!

Mary played with a musical group called 'The Camberwell Orchestra'. She played the flute and the cello with this orchestra, but not both at the same time, obviously. She would need four hands for that!

She preferred to play the flute if the concert was far from her house since it was easier to carry a flute on the bus. Her cello would get stuck in the door of the bus!

She was glad she did not play her tuba in the orchestra. It was a HUGE instrument; so HUGE that she had to keep it in a shed in her garden as it would not fit inside her house!

Mary could also make music even without any instruments; she just used whatever was nearby. She would empty all the tins out of her cupboards (or Martha's cupboards if she was visiting her friend).

She would then use the tins like a set of drums. She used wooden spoons for drumsticks.

"I love my kitchen drum kit", she said as she played "and I think the food inside tastes even more delicious after it has been used to make music!"

She found that, when she hit her drums, each tin made a different sound depending upon what it had inside:

- Tomato tins made a squishy sound, like squishy tomatoes
- Sweetcorn tins made a lovely, sweet sound
- Tins of beans made a loud 'PARP' like a pumpie
- Tins of peas made a tinkling sound, just like someone doing a pee-pee! *(Get it? ... pee-pee sounds like pea-pea)*

If Mary wanted to play a harp she would stretch elastic bands over an old shoebox. Plucking the coloured bands made a nice 'TWANG' noise.

If she needed a trumpet, she would take the cardboard tube from the inside of her kitchen paper roll. She put it to her lips and made "BRRPPP" noises. It vibrated down the tube and made a great sound.

Mary would sometime cut holes along the side of the tube to make a pretend-flute.

She would make a water-keyboard by filling bottles with different amounts of water. The different levels in the bottles produced different notes when she hit them with her wooden spoons.

(You should try making some of these instruments yourself)

(You and your friends could make a great band!)

Chapter 6

Miggly Magic

One day, while Mary was visiting her house, Martha told her about a new spell she had discovered. She called it the 'Miggly Spell'.

"Watch this", she told Mary.

She made herself magical and waved her tail in the air while shouting:

"Miggly Marrot!"

Suddenly Martha changed into a parrot!

She flew around the room and landed on top of the wardrobe.

Mary was surprised and clapped her hands with delight. She was not so pleased when Martha Parrot did a big, splashy parrot-poo on her head!

After a few minutes Martha changed back into a mouse and said:

"Oops! Sorry about that, Mary!"

She explained to Mary that the spell had to rhyme with the name of the animal she wanted to become.

"Try another one", cried Mary excitedly.

"OK, let's see ……..

Miggly Morse!"

(Which animal do you think she turned into?)

That's right, Martha turned into a horse! She was so big that she banged her head on the ceiling. Luckily, Martha did not do a poo while she was transformed into a horse because their poos are ENORMOUS.

When she turned back to normal Martha rubbed her sore head which had banged into the ceiling. She said to Mary that she had better wait until she was outside before trying "Miggly Miraffe".

"If I turned into a giraffe, I would be far too tall to fit in the house", she explained.

"Try being a dog", said Mary, so Martha waved her tail again and shouted:

"Miggly Mog!"

To Mary's surprise, she saw in front of her, not a waggy-tailed puppy dog but a green, slimy creature with bulging eyes and huge back legs.

Her friend had turned into a FROG, not a DOG!

Martha the Frog hopped about the kitchen and landed in the fish-bowl along with her pet goldfish. Mary had to scoop her out of the water with a spoon before she turned back into a mouse again!

When she eventually did turn back into a mouse, Martha said:

"I haven't really got the hang of the 'Miggly Spell' properly yet."

"Oh well, at least if you make a mistake, the spell doesn't last very long", said Mary.

"It would be good to be able to control how long each spell lasts", said Martha, "then I could choose how long I stayed transformed into the different animal".

Martha remembered that her Granny had said that she would need to discover how her magic worked all by herself.

She knew that she would have to keep practising … but first of all she would have to get dried after her swim in the gold-fish bowl.

Chapter 7

More Miggly Magic

Martha kept on practising the 'Miggly Spell' and soon discovered that she could control how long she stayed as the new animal.

If she whispered the spell quietly she only changed for a little while. If she shouted it LOUDLY, she could stay transformed for quite a long time.

She showed Mary how it worked.

"Watch this", she said to her friend.

She whispered ...

"Miggly Mebra!"

and turned into a zebra for about ten seconds.

Then she shouted:

"Miggly Mebra!"

Martha turned back into a zebra and stayed like that for a long time.

She was transformed for so long that Mary eventually had to run to the shops and ask what zebras ate for lunch!

(Zebras eat grass and the bark from trees)

This reminded Mary of her favourite joke:

- What did the dog say to the tree?
  - I like your bark!
- What did the tree say to the dog?
  - I like your bark, too!

Once Martha had turned back into a mouse, Mary told her the joke and they both had a good laugh.

The next day, Martha and Mary went to play in their local park.

Mary said that she would like to try a 'Miggly Spell' herself. The problem was that, no matter how much Mary twitched her nose, her whiskers stayed black and she did not feel any magical tingles like those Martha had told her about.

Mary just wasn't magical!

She waved her tail in the air and nothing happened. She even tried waving Martha's tail in the air but that just annoyed Martha.

"Get-out-of-it, Mary" said Martha, "Leave my tail alone!"

Then Martha had a 'good idea'.

She held Mary's right hand tightly in her left hand, waved her tail about with her right hand and became magical. Mary could feel a strange tingle in the hand which was holding on to Martha's.

Then Martha tried a 'Miggly Spell':

"Miggly Mox!"

Suddenly BOTH Martha and Mary turned into foxes!

They ran and danced and jumped all over the park and everyone was surprised to see two very jolly foxes playing in the sunshine.

By the time the spell wore off and they turned back into mice, the two friends were tired and needed to sit down on the park bench for a rest.

"That was FUN! Thanks for helping me to be a bit magical" said Mary and Martha said:

"Maybe next time you can help me to be a bit musical".

Chapter 8

Animal Rhymes

Do you remember when Martha turned into a frog instead of a dog?

Well she kept practising to get better at becoming the right animal when two names sounded the same, like 'frog' and 'dog'.

She found that if she used the 'Miggly Mat' spell, she sometimes changed into a rat or a bat or a cat!

One day she wanted to become a SWAN but turned into a PRAWN instead!

Another time when she meant to turn into a COCKATOO, she became a KANGAROO.

It was very confusing but she kept on trying, like her Granny told her to.

After a while she discovered that if she thought very, very hard about the sound the correct animal made while she cast the spell, she could make things work properly.

If she thought 'MIAOW' while saying the 'Miggly Mat' spell, she turned into a cat (most times).

There were some animals whose sounds she did not know and also a lot of animals who make the same noises as other animals.

For example, what's the difference between the squeaks made by a rat and a bat?

They both sound very similar and Martha could not tell them apart.

Fortunately, Martha did not like rats or bats so she did not want to turn into them. She concentrated on cats...

(which is a bit odd for a mouse, don't you think?)

The more animals she tried to turn into, the more confusing it became.

Sometime she found it hard to concentrate on all the things she had to do:

- First, become magical by twitching her whiskers until they glowed
- Next, wave her tail about in the air
- Then, think of the right animal noise
- And finally, say the rhyming spell

One day, Martha wanted to become a drake (which is a man-duck). She said:

"Miggly Make!"

... and she became a SNAKE instead of a drake by mistake!

(That all rhymes!)

Mary had to think quickly of a way to stop the snake from chasing her. She used some long tubes of pasta to make a set of pan-pipes.

She played some soothing music to hypnotise the snake.

Luckily the 'snake' spell did not last very long and Martha soon turned back into a mouse. She was still a bit sleepy after being hypnotised by the pan-pipe music so Mary tucked her into bed.

Mary told Martha that she was perhaps trying to become too many different animals.

"What does it matter if you become a duck or a drake?" she asked Martha.

Before Mary left to go home to her own house, she made Martha promise that she would not try any more new animals until they had BOTH checked for names which rhymed with any dangerous beasts!

(Can you think of any more rhyming animals' names?)

Chapter 9

Musical Magic

It was a rainy day in Camberwell and Mary Mouse was visiting her friend Martha. They were a bit bored because they could not go to the park since it was so wet.

"I know", said Mary, "Let's do some dancing!"

"But I can't dance", said Martha.

"Yes you can. You're good at gymnastics; well dancing is just like doing gymnastics with music. Go on; magic up some music, Martha!"

So Martha made herself magical and shouted:

"Make us some music!"

Suddenly, four people appeared in the corner of the room. One had a harp, one had a violin, one had a cello and one had a flute.

They were wearing black dinner jackets (DJs) and smart bow ties.

They started playing music by Mozart or Bach or Beethoven or someone like that.

"AARGGHH, STOP", shouted Martha,

"That's the kind of music my Grampa Jim likes!

We can't dance to that".

"Make it stop", shouted Mary.

Martha realised that she did not know how to stop one of her spells.

Then she had an idea. She decided to try saying the spell backwards. She cried out:

"Music some us make!"

... and the four musicians vanished.

Then Martha thought about the sort of music she likes and tried another spell:

"More modern music, please!"

A desk with flashing lights appeared. It had two record decks on top and there was a man behind it with headphones over his ears.

The man also wore cool sunglasses. He was called a Disc Jockey (or DJ).

He started playing disco records and Mary immediately started dancing.

Martha was a bit shy but then she remembered that Mary had said that dancing was just like gymnastics with music. She started doing star-jumps along to the beat.

Then she did head-stands and kicked her feet in the air. Soon she was not shy at all and was having a great time dancing with Mary.

Next the DJ started to play some Michael Jackson music.

"Great, that's my uncle Earl's favourite", said Mary.

Mary taught Martha how to do the moonwalk dance and they had great fun. Later, when they were tired from dancing, they had a delicious glass of orange juice with some of the leftover perkins from the mountain of biscuits which Martha had made by magic a few days before.

Martha thanked Mary for helping her to be a bit more musical and for showing her how to do the moonwalk dance.

(You should try it. You walk backwards while siding your feet along the ground.)

"Do you know", said Martha, "we had two things today called 'DJ'.

Can you remember what they were?

- *Dinner Jacket and Disc Jockey*

Mary said she could think of a third thing beginning with 'DJ' …

- Delicious Juice

Chapter 10

Tube Travel Troubles

Martha and Mary were going on an adventure!

They were going to visit Martha's distant cousin, Trevor, in Edinburgh. Now, Edinburgh is the capital of Scotland and it is very far away from London, where the two mouse friends live.

The journey involved taking a number 36 bus, then an underground train (called 'the tube') and finally a train.

The train journey alone would take over four hours and so they packed a picnic lunch of cheese and their favourite biscuits, called 'perkins'. They also took water and orange juice to drink. They packed all these goodies into two little rucksacks and set off, excitedly.

The journey started off OK with the bus arriving on time and taking them straight to the tube station. The only annoying thing was the 'announcement lady' who kept on telling everyone the name of the next stop as the bus travelled along. She also kept repeating:

'This is a number 36 bus to Queen's Park'

Mary and Martha found her especially annoying since their big ears made these announcements VERY LOUD INDEED.

When they arrived at the tube station they had to go down an escalator, which is a moving staircase. You have to step onto the stairs as they move under your feet and be ready to step off quickly at the other end. Mary had never been on an escalator before so Martha told her to hold on to the handrail. Just to be safe, Martha held Mary's other hand too.

Soon they were on the platform and the tube train came rushing into the station. There was a loud whooshing noise and a strong wind as the train approached. The wind was so strong that it nearly blew Mary's rucksack out of her hands!

The train ground to a halt and the station announcer shouted "**MIND THE GAP**" to warn everyone to be careful not to fall down between the train and the platform. But when the big doors clanged open, the mice saw a solid wall of people on the tube. There was no room to get into the carriage.

"I think we should wait for the next train", said Martha, wisely.

So they stepped back and let the train's doors close. With a loud screech, it disappeared into the dark tunnel at the other end of the station. The platform seemed strangely quiet after the tube left but soon they could hear a distant rumble as the next one approached. When its doors opened in front of the two mice, it was just the same as before; there was not much space on this carriage either.

"We'll just have to get on somehow", said Martha, "or we could be here all day! … PUSH, MARY!"

So Mary and Martha pushed the other passengers as hard as they could and managed to step onto the tube. Everyone was very squashed up.

The train driver announced: "**MIND THE DOORS**" and the big doors clanged shut again.

But, Mary's tail was still sticking out of the carriage and it got stuck in the gap between the doors.

"AYAH, AYAH, HELP, my tail is stuck!" cried Mary.

The tube train started to move with Mary's tail sticking out of the door. Her tail was going to hit the wall when the train went into the tunnel at the end of the station platform.

(Can you see her tail sticking out?)

"HELP", Mary cried, "SOMEBODY HELP!"

Quick as a flash, Martha made herself magical by twitching her nose.

As soon as her whiskers glowed, she shouted:

"Make me a mouse-hole!"

A little hole appeared in the door around Mary's tail and she managed to pull it into the carriage just as the train entered the tunnel. Her tail missed the wall by two inches!

"PHEW, that was close. Thanks Martha", she said.

"Never mind, Mary", said Martha, "We'll soon be on the train to Edinburgh and we can have a nice long sit down on comfortable seats".

But, that was not to be, as we shall find out next time!

Chapter 11

Train Travel Troubles

When Mary and Martha reached the station to catch their train to Edinburgh they were very hot and tired.

As they came back up the escalator (holding tightly on to the handrail again), Mary said: "I'm really looking forward to a nice long relaxing journey to Edinburgh".

Martha said: "Yes, we'll need to have a rest to build up our energy as cousin Trevor tells me there is a big festival on up there just now and there will be lots of shows to go to".

Mary added: "I'd like to see some music and dance shows. I've heard they have a musical instrument called the bagpipes in Scotland. I'd love to hear bagpipes and maybe even try to play them".

Martha said: "I hope to see some magic shows to get some new ideas for my spells".

When they got to the top of the escalator, there were hundreds of people in the station.

"What a lot of people" said Martha, "I hope they are not ALL going to be on our train because I know the festival in Edinburgh is very popular".

But, when they eventually found the right platform for their train to Scotland it was packed with people waiting to get on. In fact, when they got onto the train, there were no empty seats left; they were going to have to stand all the way. Four and a half hours!

"But I'm so tired!" cried Mary "I can't stand for all that time".

Then Martha had a good idea.

She saw that there was some room in the luggage racks above the seats in the carriage. She did a fantastic gymnastics flip into the air and landed right in the middle of the empty space on the rack.

"Quick Mary, come on up!" she shouted.

"I can't do gymnastics like that" said Mary "and I can't reach up there."

Martha came to the rescue.

She twitched her whiskers and cast a magic spell:

"My friend needs a ladder!"

Suddenly a ladder appeared at Mary's feet.

The top of the ladder was leaning against the luggage rack. Mary scampered up the ladder onto the rack beside Martha.

A big man with a huge fat tummy started to climb the ladder behind Mary. He was too heavy and would have squashed the two friends and may even have broken the luggage rack.

Martha wanted to cancel the ladder spell … and quickly.

(Do you remember what she must do to cancel a spell? That's right! Saying the spell backwards stops Martha's magic. So what does she need to say?)

"Ladder a needs friend my!"

The ladder disappeared before the man could reach the top.

He was left suspended in mid-air. He legs started spinning round like when Shaggy and Scooby-Doo start running in the cartoon programmes on TV.

He fell down and landed in the passageway with a BUMP!

The two friends now had plenty of room on the luggage rack and they spread out their picnic. When they had finished all their food and drinks, they were very sleepy.

"We'll need a good long sleep so we are ready for all the exciting things that cousin Trevor has planned for us", said Martha.

They snuggled down beside each other on the high luggage rack and gave each other a nice cuddle.

But before they fell asleep, they tied their train tickets to the tips of their tails and dangled them over the side of the luggage rack.

This was so that the ticket inspector did not have to wake them up when he came round to check everyone's tickets.

Clever mice!

Their dangling tickets and tails tickled the noses of some of the other passengers below and this annoyed them a lot!

Martha and Mary did not really care if the other passengers were annoyed, because:

A. These people were lucky enough to have seats, so they should not really complain

B. The two mice friends were fast asleep, dreaming of festival fun to come.

Chapter 12

Festival Fun

When the train pulled into Edinburgh station, Martha's cousin Trevor and his friend Declan were waiting on the platform.

Now, for those of you who don't already know, Trevor is known as *'The Rabbit with Three Ears'* because he is a rabbit and he has three ears. Declan is also a rabbit, but he has ten ears.

These two have been friends for a long time and get up to lots of adventures together.

When Martha spotted Trevor on the platform, she shouted "Hi Trevor. Here we are!". Trevor ran over and offered to help them with their rucksacks but the mice said they were not heavy as they had eaten all of their food and had drunk all of their drinks too.

Then the cousins introduced their friends to each other.

"Martha and Mary, meet Declan", said Trevor

"Pleased to meet you", they said.

"Trevor and Declan, meet Mary", said Martha

"Pleased to meet you too" they replied.

"Right, let's go and see what's happening in the Festival City", said Declan whose ten ears were tied up with two ribbons: one white and the other blue, like the Scottish flag.

As soon as they walked up the long steep ramp from the station to the street they heard a very loud screeching sound.

"MMMWWWEHHHH, MMMWWWEHHHH"

"What on Earth is that noise?" asked Martha.

"Oh, that's the bagpipes", said Trevor "Isn't it dreadful? I think they sound like a cat with its tail stuck in a door."

"That's right", said Declan, "It sounds just like our friend, Ginger George, in a lot of pain."

"MMMWWWEHHHH, MMMWWWEHHHH"

went the bagpipes.

"Where is it coming from?" asked Martha.

"Over there, look!" said Declan. Sure enough, across the road stood a young girl dressed in Scottish tartan from head to toe playing the bagpipes.

"It looks like she's being attacked by an octopus", said Martha.

"I don't like it … " said Mary. " … I love it!" she added; her little eyes wide open with wonder and excitement. She started to dance along the pavement in time to the music.

Everyone was amazed to see Mary doing some of her coolest dance moves.

"You'd think she'd be embarrassed", said Trevor, in a loud voice.

"SSSHHHH!" said Martha, giving the two rabbits an angry stare, "Mary's enjoying herself, and it's good to stretch after a long train journey."

Martha joined in with some of her 'gym' stretches to ease her muscles which were still a bit stiff.

The girl played lots of tunes on the bagpipes as more and more people joined in the dancing.

Trevor and Declan did NOT join in.

Martha looked round at the two rabbits and saw that they were stuffing things into their pockets.

"What's all that?" she asked.

"Oh, just some of our ears", said Trevor.

(You may not know this but Trevor and Declan can take their ears off if they want to; and at this time they REALLY wanted to!)

"The bagpipes are too loud so we have taken off some of our ears so we can't hear them so much", he added.

"That's not very nice", she said, but she was smiling at the two crazy rabbits.

Soon the girl finished playing and everyone clapped their hands. Except Trevor and Declan who were quickly sticking their ears back on before Mary noticed.

Mary was busy telling the girl how much she loved the sound of the bagpipes and was delighted when the girl asked her if she would like to try playing them.

(I'm quite sure that the girl did not expect Mary to be able to play them but, of course, she did not know how good the little mouse was at making music from strange objects.)

Soon Mary was playing some of her favourite songs. 'Yellow Submarine' sounded a bit strange on the bagpipes but everyone seemed to like it.

They all started to dance along to Mary's music too.

Even Trevor and Declan joined in this time.

They were used to dancing with their rabbit chorus … but their dancing was not normally accompanied by bagpipe music!

Chapter 13

Further Festival Fun

When Mary had finished playing all of her favourite tunes, she thanked the girl for the loan of her bagpipes and handed them back.

"Right", said Trevor, "What would you like to do now?"

"Music and dancing!" said Mary.

"Magic and Illusions!" said Martha.

"OK, let's see what shows we can find", said Declan.

The four friends wandered up the hill from the station to the Royal Mile where there are lots of famous old buildings.

One of these buildings contains the Scottish Storytelling Centre. Many different shows can be seen in its theatre during the festival: including plays, storytelling (of course) and poetry.

They looked at the list of all the various shows and picked out two which fitted what the mice wanted to see.

Martha's uncle Daniel works in the centre so he made sure they got good seats for the shows.

First they went to a 'Flamenco' show.

Flamenco is a type of dance from Spain which involves stamping your feet and clapping your hands ... a lot!

There were two ladies in brightly coloured, frilly dresses and a man in smart black trousers and a jazzy shirt. They all stamped and clapped along to the music which was played by a young man with a Spanish guitar.

Mary was itching to join in but she did not like to interrupt the dancers. At the end of the show they announced that anyone who wanted to try Flamenco could come onto the stage and join them. Mary was off like a shot; clapping and stamping, twisting and turning.

Martha remembered what Mary had said about dancing just being like 'gymnastics with music' so she did some of her stretching exercises in time with the guitar playing.

Trevor and Declan just stayed in their seats.

They had not heard the invitation to join in because all of their ears were stuffed into their pockets (again)!

Next, the four friends went to a Magic Show.

It was not REAL magic like Martha does, of course. It was just card tricks and other illusions. But it was very slick and no-one could see how the magician did the tricks.

He was showing off a lot; waving his hands in the air and shouting:

"ABRACADABRA"

Near the end of his show, he asked for a volunteer from the audience to help with a card trick.

Trevor went up on stage and picked a card from a normal pack. He had a look at his card and it was the '3 of Hearts'.

He showed it to the audience so they knew what it was but did not show it to the magician.

Then Trevor put his card back into the pack and the magician shuffled them and pretended to say a magic spell.

He shouted:

"ABRACADABRA"

… again!

What he did not know was that Martha had secretly made herself magical and whispered her REAL spell:

"Meddle with the cards!"

The magician handed Trevor his card back and announced "Please show everyone your card. It's the 3 of Hearts".

But when Trevor showed his card to the audience it was one from a completely different pack of cards.

It was 'Peg-Leg Percy' from the game 'Pirate Snap'.

Everyone laughed and the magician was really confused.

"But … but … it WAS the 3 of Hearts", he cried.

The poor magician scratched his head and wondered what could have gone wrong with his trick.

"That's never happened before", he sighed.

The four friends said 'goodbye' to Martha's uncle Daniel and left the Storytelling Centre in search of some lunch.

Trevor and Declan had no idea why the magician's trick had gone wrong but they both thought it was very funny.

Mary and Martha just smiled knowingly at each other.

Chapter 14

Café Chaos

"Where shall we have lunch? I'm starving", said Mary as soon as they left the Storytelling Centre after their dancing and magic shows.

"I know a great little café at the top of Leith Walk which is very close to my house", said Declan, "We can eat in the café then go back to my place for a rest. We could watch a programme on the TV if you want".

They all agreed that this was a good idea.

In the café, Martha ordered a bowl of tomato soup and Mary asked for fish-fingers with baked beans. The two rabbits said they were not very hungry so Trevor just ordered some chocolate ice-cream and Declan said that he wanted apple-crumble and custard.

There was haggis on the menu but the two London mice did not want to try it ...

(which is a shame because it's really yummy).

Very soon the lady shouted to tell them that their food was ready. It was one of those cafés where they don't bring your food to the table; you have to collect it from the counter. Trevor and Declan said that they would go and get it.

First they brought Mary and Martha's lunch over and told them to start eating while they collected their own food. On the way back to the table, Declan spilled some of his custard on the floor but he did not notice it.

Trevor did not notice the custard on the floor either. He stood on it and skidded forward, banging into Declan!

Trevor's ice-cream went up in the air and landed on Declan's neck.

It was so cold, it made Declan throw his bowl into the air too.

The apple-crumble and what was left of his custard landed on Trevor's face.

(Luckily, it was not too hot).

Both rabbits now skidded forward and fell over the table where Martha and Mary were eating their lunch.

Their faces were pushed right into their food. Martha's face was covered in tomato soup and Mary had beans and fish-fingers squashed into hers.

"Oops, sorry" said the two rabbits and they all started to giggle.

The café owner was NOT pleased. He told the four of them to leave the café immediately.

"GET-OUT-OF-IT!", he shouted.

The four friends apologised for the mess and ran outside, remembering to leave the money to pay for their ruined lunches.

Now, it rains a lot in Edinburgh, especially during the festival time.

When they got outside the rain was pouring down.

Martha thought that she would magic up some umbrellas.

She was still not sure that she wanted the two rabbits to know about her magic just yet, so she started to twitch her nose to make herself magical without letting them see her.

Luckily, before anyone noticed her glowing whiskers, Trevor had one of his 'good ideas'.

"Why don't we just let the rain wash all the food off of us?" he said.

So, that's what they did. They just ran about in the rain until they were clean.

Soon, the rain was falling so hard that the street was like a river. Leith Walk is on a steep hill so the water was flowing quickly downhill.

Trevor had another 'good idea'.

He found an empty box at the back door of the café. The box had been used to deliver eggs and was not needed anymore.

He put the box in the rain-river and told the others to jump in.

They all jumped into the eggbox-boat and sailed down Leith Walk.

"Wee-Hee!" cried Trevor.

"Yahoo!" shouted Declan.

They were going at such a speed that Mary was a bit scared so Martha put her arm around her to make her feel safe.

Half-way down the hill, the box banged into the pavement at the end of Declan's street and came to a sploshy stop.

The friends all jumped out and ran along to Declan's house, dumping the wet box in the recycling bin as they went.

Once inside the house, Declan gave them all towels to dry themselves.

They realised that they had not had any lunch so Trevor looked in Declan's food cupboard where he found some tins of soup.

"You can choose from chicken broth or tomato soup", he said.

"Anything but tomato soup", said Martha, "I've had enough of that for today, thanks!"

She remembered it dripping off of her face in the café.

After lunch, the four friends played a game of 'Ladders and Snakes'.

(Do you remember how to play that game?)

You play it just like 'Snakes and Ladders' but you move <u>up</u> the snakes and <u>down</u> the ladders.

Chapter 15

Head Cold

A few days later Mary and Martha were back home in London.

Their train journey back to London was much better; it was not so busy and they managed to find seats. The tube and bus were also a lot quieter and Mary did not get her tail stuck in the door this time.

Mary thanked Martha for taking her to Scotland to meet the two rabbits.

"Your cousin Trevor is very nice and his friend Declan is lovely!" said Mary, "And Edinburgh is a wonderful city. We must go back to visit more of Scotland one day".

(I'm sure they will!)

"Yes", agreed Martha, "We must try to see more of Trevor and Declan in the future. It's difficult when they live so far away".

When they got to Camberwell they said 'goodnight' to each other and carried their little rucksacks home.

Martha was not really feeling very well. Her head was sore and her eyes looked a bit red in her bathroom mirror.

"I hope I'm not becoming ill", she thought, "My Granny says that you can catch a cold from getting very wet".

She remembered how they had all been running about outside in the rain in Edinburgh.

Martha unpacked her rucksack and put her soggy clothes into the washing machine.

She looked at the little model of Greyfriars Bobby which she had bought to remind her of her holiday in Scotland.

Then she got into bed and snuggled down to sleep.

Next morning she felt even worse. Her head was still sore and her nose was completely blocked. She decided it would be best to stay in bed so she tried to make a spell to get a cup of tea made. But when she tried to say "Make me a nice cup of tea", her nose was so blocked it sounded like:

"Nake ne a nice nup of nea"

… so nothing happened.

No matter how hard she tried, she could not say the letter 'M'.

(You try saying 'M' while holding your nose.)

Then she remembered that her spells worked with the letter 'W' when she was upside-down. So she stood on her head in the middle of the bed and said:

"Why, I'd love a cup of tea ...

to be on the table beside the bed!"

She added the bit about the tea being on the table because the last time she magicked up a drink when she was upside-down, it appeared in her hand and poured all over her.

Suddenly, the cup of tea was sitting on the table beside her and she turned around to be the right way up again so she could drink it. It was lovely!

Her head was too sore to do head-stands anymore so she decided she could not make any more upside-down spells.

Anyway, her nose was so red and sore from blowing it that she found it hard to twitch it to become magical in the first place.

"How will I get my lunch without magic?" she wondered.

Just then the phone rang.

It was her friend Mary calling to see if she was OK. When Mary heard Martha speaking she knew she was very ill. Mary said she would come round to help.

The first thing Mary did when she arrived was make another pot of tea for both of them. She thought Martha should have sweet tea so she decided to put some sugar in Martha's cup.

She saw a big bowl beside the cooker so Mary added two spoonfuls and stirred it in.

When Martha drank it she immediately spat it out again.

"YUK!" she said "That's horrible. Are you trying to kill me, Mary?"

What Mary did not know was that the bowl of white stuff beside the cooker was SALT, not SUGAR!

"Sorry Martha. There's still plenty tea in the pot. I'll pour you a fresh cup" said Mary.

"Without sugar or salt, this time" said Martha grumpily.

Mary tucked Martha up in bed again and wrapped her own green ribbon around her friend's neck beside the yellow one she already had on.

"There, that will keep you nice and cosy until you feel better" she said. Martha had a snooze in her bed and Mary went back into the kitchen to make their lunch.

While she was there, she stuck labels on all the jars and bowls to tell people what was in each of them. She did not want any more mix-ups.

After lunch, Mary played some quiet, soothing music on some home-made instruments.

She shook a box of cornflakes like a rattle in one hand.

Then she nibbled little holes into a bar of chocolate to make a harmonica.

Martha soon dozed off and slept for most of the day.

Mary decided she would stay the night in Martha's spare room to look after her friend while she was ill.

There was not much food in Martha's cupboards since they had been away to Scotland on holiday so Mary ate the chocolate harmonica for her dinner.

It was yummy!

Chapter 16

Supermarket Surprise

It was Martha's birthday and her friend Mary gave her a present. It was beautifully wrapped in yellow tissue paper (Martha's favourite colour).

Martha was excited as she ripped open the parcel. Inside the wrapping paper was a little square box and inside the box was a lovely new bangle.

It was very shiny and had an unusual pattern of black and white stripes on it; like a zebra's skin.

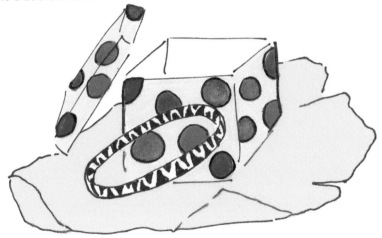

Martha was delighted with it and thanked Mary for her kindness.

"I'm going to wear it all day", she told her friend.

Later in the day, Martha was going to the shops to buy something for her lunch. Although she is magical, she remembered her Granny telling her that it was unfair to use her magic to get food when other people had to buy it.

(She also remembered the time she magicked up a hundred perkins by mistake!)

She skipped along to the local supermarket wondering what she could eat for her special lunch.

"They have so many delicious things there", she thought to herself.

By the time she got there, she had chosen.

"I'll buy some nice red cheddar cheese and a juicy red apple", she thought and she put these two things into her shopping basket.

When she got to the check-out, there were quite a few people queuing, waiting to pay so she decided to use the 'self-checkouts'. These are the machines which allow you to scan the things you are buying and put money into a slot to pay for them. They save you having to wait for a person to serve you.

Martha likes these machines because they are very polite.

The machines say:

"If you have a loyalty card, please scan it now"

and

"Thank you for shopping with us. Goodbye"

She scanned her cheese and apple and pressed the button to say she was finished. She was very surprised to see that her shopping cost £200!

There must be a mistake; two things for your lunch cannot cost £200, even in London!

She cancelled everything and tried again but still it came up with £200 for her two lunch items. She was very confused.

She called over one of the shop assistant ladies to see if she could help. The lady agreed that £200 seemed a lot of money for some cheese and an apple.

They started again with Martha scanning and the lady watching what she was doing. Very soon, the lady knew what was happening.

As Martha was scanning the food, the machine was reading the black and white lines on her new bangle like a barcode.

This barcode just happened to match a very expensive item in the supermarket and was charging her £100 every time she scanned it.

Martha started again, this time scanning the food with her other hand (which did not have the bangle on it).

It came to £3.45 this time, which is still expensive for cheese and an apple.

But, London is an expensive place to live.

Martha put her money into the machine and thanked it when it told her to 'have a nice day'.

She skipped all the way home and had a lovely birthday lunch.

After lunch, Martha went to visit Mary at her house nearby. Mary had baked a special birthday cake for Martha. It was a chocolate cake and it had birthday candles on top. Mary lit the candles and was about to sing 'Happy Birthday to You' to her friend when Martha remembered what had happened that morning.

She told Mary about the trouble she had had at the supermarket with her new bangle working like a barcode. Mary thought this was a very funny story and she laughed so much that she blew out the candles on Martha's cake by mistake.

When she stopped laughing, Mary relit the candles and sang the birthday song. As she blew out the candles, Martha made a birthday wish and hoped it would come true.

(I wonder what Martha wished for. Do you?)

Chapter 17

The Not-Lazy Lion

One day, Martha was feeling very happy and wanted to thank Mary for being a good friend and giving her such a lovely birthday present.

"How would you like a day out at the zoo?" said Martha.

"That would be great!" said Mary excitedly.

The two friends set off for London Zoo and were soon wandering about looking at lots of different animals. Mary liked the pink fluffy flamingos and tried copying them by standing on one leg. She could not do it for very long and kept falling over.

When they came to the lion enclosure there was a huge crowd of people all looking in.

There were five lions in there; four of them were walking about roaring at each other and at the crowd. But one lion just lay on the ground, doing nothing.

A little boy shouted:

"Look at that lazy lion. Come on Lazy-bones, get up".

Another boy shouted:

"Yeah, stop just lyin' there".

He was very pleased at his own joke because 'lyin'' sounds like 'lion'.

Some people laughed but Mary and Martha did not, they both thought that the boys were very rude and cheeky.

"That lion doesn't look very happy", said Martha to her friend,

"I wonder why he is so sad".

There was a zoo-keeper nearby and Martha asked her what was wrong with that lion.

"We don't really know", she said, "he was fine until last week then he stopped eating and now he just lies about all day".

"Well, why don't you ask him what's wrong?" said Martha.

"But, nobody here understands lion-talk. Lions are big cats and are a bit like other cats. The only thing small cats can say is 'MYEH' and everything lions say sounds like:

'ROAAAARRRRR'.

"I'd like to go in and try to speak to him", said Martha.

"You'd be like Daniel", said Mary.

"Who? My uncle Daniel in Edinburgh?" asked Martha.

"No, Silly! *'Daniel in the Lions' Den'* from my storybook", Mary replied.

"Brave Daniel went into a den to stay with some lions and was not hurt by them", she explained, "I hope you'll be safe too".

The zoo-keeper was not happy about Martha going into the enclosure.

"The lions might eat a mouse", she said.

"Ah, but they would not eat another lion", replied Martha.

She made herself magical, waved her tail in the air and shouted:

"Miggly Mion!"

She turned into a lion in front of Mary and the zoo-keeper.

The zoo-keeper was a bit surprised, but Mary told her not to worry, it was still Martha really. She explained about the magic and asked the zoo-keeper to keep their secret.

"If it helps that poor, sad lion, I promise not to tell anyone", she said.

The two cheeky boys were not so brave now that there was a lion OUTSIDE the enclosure, beside them. They ran away crying for their mummies. The zoo-keeper opened the gate to the lion enclosure and Martha walked in.

She went up to the lyin' lion and said:

"Hello, I'm Martha Mouse … I mean Martha Lion … pleased to meet you".

The lion looked up sadly and said 'Oh Hi. I'm Laurie Lion".

"Why are you sad, Laurie? You look as if you have not eaten for a while".

"That's just it. They keep on giving me meat to eat and I've decided I want to be a vegetarian now. All the other lions are happy to eat my dinner but I don't know how to tell the zoo-keepers what I want to eat. They don't seem to understand me" said the lion, sadly.

"OK, tell me what you'd like and I'll tell the zoo-keeper" said Martha.

The lion started listing all the lovely things he'd like to eat and Martha listened carefully. Luckily she had a good memory and could remember all the things he wanted.

Just to be sure, Martha made it into a sort of poem to help her remember it. The list was:

- Carrots and beans, potatoes and greens
- Bananas and pears and grapes
- Peaches with custard
- Brown bread with mustard
- And pasta in all different shapes

Martha told him that she would pass on the message to the zoo-keeper.

She walked over to the gate and just as she got to it her magic spell wore off and she turned back into a mouse.

She told the zoo-keeper that the lion did not want to eat meat anymore and that she had a list of goodies he wanted instead.

Do you remember any of the things on the list?

It was:

- Carrots and beans, potatoes and greens
- Bananas and pears and grapes
- Peaches with custard
- Brown bread with mustard
- And pasta in all different shapes

The lion got all the food he wanted and he did not have to share it with the other lions because they still preferred to eat meat.

The not-lazy lion soon had a tummy full of yummy veggie food was back running about with his friends and everyone was happy.

Chapter 18

Special Invitations

There was great excitement!

The postman had brought Martha a special letter; it was from the Queen! Her hands were shaking as she opened the envelope.

The letter said:

Her Majesty the Queen is pleased to invite

Martha Mouse

to a Royal Garden Party at Buckingham Palace

You may bring a guest

Please dress smartly

Martha decided she would invite Mary as her guest so she phoned her to tell her the news. But Mary had exciting news too; she was ALSO invited!

"If we can both bring a guest, why don't we ask your cousin Trevor and his friend Declan to come with us", said Mary.

"Good idea, Mary", said Martha.

Martha phoned Cousin Trevor to tell him about the invitation.

"That's great", he said, "Declan and I will wear our kilts".

"And Martha and I will buy new hats", she replied.

That afternoon, Mary and Martha visited some very posh shops in Oxford Street to look for hats. They were having great fun trying on lots of different types.

There were wide hats that looked like big dinner plates, tall hats that looked like chimneys and tiny little ones that you could hardly see.

Some hats had flowers and bows; others had feathers and long dangly ribbons.

The mice had to be careful to choose hats which would fit between their large ears. Martha said she could cut two holes in the wide hat and stick her ears through them. This made Mary giggle.

Finally, Mary saw a lovely orange, furry hat on the shop counter and picked it up to try it on. When she plopped it on her head, it jumped right up in the air and let out a loud SCREEEEECH.

It was not a hat at all; it was the shopkeeper's cat!

The cat had been sleeping on the counter and was very angry at having been woken up. It started hissing and chased Mary around the shop.

(Cats like chasing mice.

But do you know an animal that likes to chase cats?

That's right!

Dogs like to chase cats.)

Martha wiggled her nose and cast a 'Miggly Spell' ...

"Miggly Mog!"

She remembered to think hard about the noise a dog makes so that she did not turn into a FROG like she did before. She turned into a large dog and chased the cat out of the door.

Mary was safe again.

When the spell wore off and Martha became a mouse again, the shopkeeper asked them both to leave; politely but firmly.

She didn't say:

"GET-OUT-OF-IT!"

like the café owner in Edinburgh had shouted when he chucked them out.

The hat-shop owner was very posh and said:

"I must respectfully request that you two ladies vacate these premises".

They ran out of the shop, laughing and giggling.

"These hats are much too fancy, anyway", said Mary.

"A bit 'faffy-foo' as my granny would say", agreed Martha, "And far too expensive", she added.

The next day, they went to a local market in Camden and bought lovely hats in their favourite colours.

(Do you remember which colours they like?)

Martha's hat was YELLOW and Mary's hat was GREEN.

Chapter 19

Travel to London

The day before the Royal Garden Party, Trevor and Declan flew down from Edinburgh in Trevor's helicopter.

As they approached London, they could see lots of famous buildings. The two rabbits recognised many of them from seeing pictures in a book they had bought.

They saw:

- The London Eye
  - Which is a huge big wheel that you can ride upon in little carriages
- The Gherkin
  - Which is a large glass building that sticks up in the air and looks like a … well … like a huge gherkin
- The Tower of London
  - Where baddies were sent to jail in the olden-days
- Tower Bridge
  - Which is a big road bridge over the river Thames that opens up to let tall ships pass underneath
- The Shard
  - Which is like a big glass spike scratching the sky

(Can you find these 5 famous landmarks on the next page?)

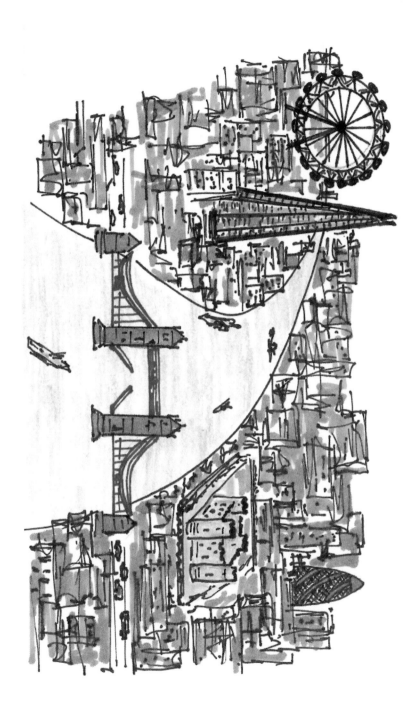

Trevor was so busy staring at Tower Bridge to see if it would open that he nearly crashed his helicopter into the Shard.

"Watch where you're going, Trevor", shouted Declan.

As they flew over Buckingham Palace, they could see lots of open, green space around it. Declan said "That's where the party is being held. I wonder if the Queen will let us park the helicopter in her garden; there's plenty of room".

Just then a little red warning light began to flash on the dashboard of the helicopter.

"We're just about to find out about the parking, Declan. We're running out of petrol. HOLD ON!" cried Trevor. The helicopter swooped down and made an emergency landing on the front garden of Buckingham Palace where a little, old lady was cutting the grass.

"I think that's the Queen", said Declan, "Look, she has a crown on her head!"

The Queen came over and said, "Can one help you, gentlemen?"

Trevor and Declan bowed very low and all their ears lay on the grass which the Queen had been cutting. When they stood up straight again they were all covered in little bits of grass. The Queen was very kind and tried not to laugh but she did have a little smile on her face.

"Sorry, Your Majesty, we've run out of petrol and had to make an emergency landing", said Trevor.

"Well", she replied, "If you two would cut the rest of One's grass, One could give you some petrol from One's lawnmower".

(That's the funny way the Queen speaks, calling herself 'One').

The two rabbits took the lawnmower and cut the grass while the Queen sat on a golden deckchair and had a glass of wine.

(Well, she is the Queen after all.)

When all the grass was cut, she gave them some petrol for the helicopter.

"Thank you, Your Majesty", they said

The two rabbits bowed very low again and got even more grass cuttings on their ears. This time, the Queen could not stop herself and she burst out laughing.

Trevor and Declan got back into the helicopter and flew on towards Martha's house.

Although Martha has a parking space outside her house it was not big enough for Trevor's helicopter. As they approached Camberwell, they saw a building with a large letter 'H' pained on the roof.

"That's a helicopter landing pad", said Declan, "can't we can land there?"

"Not really," replied Trevor, "that building is a hospital and the landing space is needed for emergency ambulance helicopters". So they landed on Camberwell Green nearby and walked the rest of the way to Martha's house.

They saw a fish-and-chip shop on the corner as they walked along and decided to buy some for their dinner. They noticed some things were different between London and Edinburgh chip-shops:

- There were different kinds of fish, not just haddock
- You could get mushy peas *(What!)*
- There was no 'chippy' sauce, just vinegar!
- They gave you little wooden forks to eat your chips with

"Very strange", they thought as they shared their 'suppers' with Mary and Martha.

Trevor said he could hardly understand what the man in the chip-shop was saying because of his strong London accent and Mary said:

"Pardon? What did you say? I could not understand your strong Scottish accent!"

They all laughed at her joke.

Chapter 20

Martha's Medal

The next day was the day of the Royal Garden Party. Trevor and Declan were sharing Martha's spare bedroom and both woke up very excited.

Mary had come round to have breakfast with the others and they talked about their plans for the day. The Garden Party was not until the afternoon so they all decided to take an open-top bus tour around London to see all the important sights.

The four friends managed to get seats at the front of the bus, upstairs so they had a great view.

There were lots of statues of famous men and women all trying to look important, which it is hard to do with a seagull standing on your head. (As Trevor knew from experience).

They saw all the buildings which Trevor and Declan has seen from the air in the helicopter *(Do you remember what they were?)*

After a while, their bus was crossing over Tower Bridge when it suddenly stopped. The driver got out and was looking under the bonnet at the engine. He poked a few things and turned some knobs but nothing worked; the engine would not start.

Suddenly, they heard a loud blast from the horn of a tall ship which was sailing down the river. It was too tall to fit under the bridge so the bridge had to be opened. The road in the middle of the bridge split apart and started to rise up in the air. The bus was still on the bridge and started to rise up too!

The driver shouted "HELP!" and ran away down the slope to get off of the bridge but the passengers did not have time to follow him, they were clinging on to the backs of the seats in front of them as the slope got steeper and steeper.

Martha immediately jumped up and ran down the stairs of the bus, making herself magical as she went. She sat on the driver's seat and shouted:

"Mechanical Magic!

Fix this engine!"

The engine burst into life and the bus was able to move. By this time the gap in the bridge was as wide as the tips of your fingers when your arms are stretched out fully!

(Stretch out your arms to see how wide the gap was!)

The gap was quickly getting wider and wider as the bridge opened up more and more.

Martha pressed her foot hard on the pedal to make the bus go as fast as it could. It zoomed up the slope of the bridge towards the gap.

She shouted, **"Hang on tight"** to everyone as the bus reached the top of the slope. The bus flew into the air and across the gap.

It landed on the other side with a slight thump and Martha pressed the brake to make it slow down.

When it stopped on the other side of the bridge everyone was cheering and clapping.

"Well done Martha", said Mary and gave her a big hug.

The friends decided it was time to go home to get ready for the Garden Party so they took a taxi back to Martha's house. (They had had enough of buses for one day). They asked the taxi driver to wait for them while they quickly got changed into their party clothes. Trevor and Declan looked very smart in their tartan kilts and Mary and Martha looked great in their new hats.

When they arrived at Buckingham Palace, there were crowds of people outside the gates and the four friends were very proud as they showed their tickets to the uniformed guard and were let inside. Hundreds of people were milling about drinking wine or orange juice or tea or whatever they wanted! They were given little sandwiches with the crusts cut off and sausages on sticks to eat. It was all yummy food!

Then there was a little fanfare on a trumpet and the Queen herself appeared. Everyone was very quiet as she stepped up onto a little stage to make a speech.

"Firstly, One would like to thank you all for coming today and One hopes you have noticed how nicely One's grass has been cut". She looked over to Trevor and Declan and gave a little nod.

"One is particularly pleased to see that you have managed to get it off of your many ears, Gentlemen", she added. The two rabbits' faces went very red at this point.

"Now, One would like to give special thanks to a guest who has been particularly brave recently. Would Martha Mouse care to come forward please?"

Martha was surprised to hear the Queen mention her name but she walked up to the stage. The crowd started to clap although most of them had no idea who Martha was or what she had done.

The Queen told them all about the incident with the bus on Tower Bridge.

She said that the bus driver who ran away had been locked up in the Tower of London but that she planned to let him out as soon as he said that he was sorry.

Then, a lady stepped forward with a blue velvet cushion in her hands. On the cushion there was a gold medal with the words **"FOR BRAVERY"** written on it.

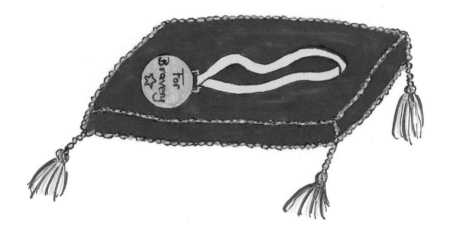

The Queen took the medal and hung it around Martha's neck by the yellow ribbon which was attached to it.

The crowd cheered and whooped and Martha did a little curtsey to the Queen and went back to join her friends.

Martha was very happy with her medal.

Chapter 21

Hallowe'en Party

Martha and Mary were going to a Hallowe'en Party run by their local library. Lots of people from Camberwell were going to be there.

Like most Hallowe'en parties, it was 'fancy dress' which meant everyone had to come dressed up as something scary.

The two friends had great fun deciding what they would dress up as.

Martha decided she would be a witch (since she can do magic).

Her costume was a black cloak and a tall hat.

She cut two holes in the brim of the hat to let her ears stick through.

She also had a magic wand.

The wand did not really work but she had fun pretending that it did.

Mary put a sheet over her head to become a scary ghost.

At first, she kept on banging into things because she could not see where she was going.

Martha helped her to cut two little holes in the sheet where her eyes would be.

Mary could then see out.

"WOOOOOOO", said Mary, practicing her scary ghost voice.

At the party, they played a lot of traditional Hallowe'en games.

Firstly, there were treacle scones hanging from bits of string and they had to try to eat them without using their hands. The scones were dripping with black treacle so all their faces got very sticky and messy.

Next, came 'Bobbing for Apples' (or 'Dooking for Apples' as Martha's Scottish cousin, Trevor, would call it). Here, they had to try to catch apples which were floating in a bowl of water on the floor.

There were two ways of playing this game:

1. Martha kneeled in front of the bowl and tried to bite the apples. Every time she tried to bite an apple it would just float away. She had to put her face under the water and push the apples down to the bottom of the bowl. Then she could bite an apple and bring it out of the bowl to loads of cheering and a lot of dripping water.
2. Mary did not want to get soaking wet so she chose to stand on a chair holding the end of a fork in her mouth over the bowl of apples. She would let the fork drop and try to spear an apple. After a few attempts, she became quite good at it.

It was lucky that there were two different bowls of apples, one for each way of playing the game. Otherwise, Mary might have dropped the fork onto the back of Martha's head, which would not be very funny!

Now, there was a boy at the party who was not very nice. When people were playing the game Martha's way, he would push their heads down into the bowl of water. He thought this was great fun but everyone else soon got fed up with him.

His name was 'Peter' but Mary called him 'Peter, the cheater' or 'Pete, the cheat' for short. She called him this because he always tried to find a way to cheat at any game they played.

'Pete, the cheat' had come dressed as a devil. He had a red costume with a pointy tail and a red mask with horns.

"It really suits him", said Mary, "He is a bit of a devil himself".

Later on they played 'Musical Chairs'. Mary provided the music, of course. It was beautiful and no-one knew which instrument she was playing because it was under her ghost-sheet and they could not see it.

Even here, 'Pete, the cheat' was a pest. He thought it would be a great idea to tie a little chair to his bottom with a piece of string.

This meant that, whenever Mary stopped the music, he just sat down wherever he was while everyone else was running around trying to find a chair.

"Hey, that's not fair", someone shouted.

"That's cheating", said another.

Martha decided that she was fed-up with Peter. He was spoiling everyone else's fun and she thought she'd use some magic to pay him back. She secretly made herself magical by twitching her nose and said:

"Maybe that chair needs new legs!"

Instantly, the four legs on Peter's chair turned into breadsticks. He did not notice until the next time Mary stopped the music. He sat down quickly and the four breadstick snapped into lots of tiny pieces.

They were not strong enough to hold his weight. Pete fell over and landed in one of the apple bowls.

The water sploshed all over his body and he had to go home to get dried and change his clothes.

Martha told everyone that her magic wand really worked and had magicked up the breadsticks but no-one really believed her.

Only Mary knew how the breadsticks had really appeared.

Everyone was happy because 'Pete, the cheat' was no longer ruining the party.

He did come back later to say 'sorry' to everyone (and to collect his party-bag of goodies, of course!)

Chapter 22

Mary Makes a Mess

One day, Mary decided she wanted to try being magical, just like Martha.

She had tried before but it just did not work.

Then she remembered the time when Martha had used the 'Miggly Spell' to change them BOTH into foxes. It had worked because they were holding hands when the spell was cast.

Mary wondered if this would work for her too.

She waited until Martha was having a snooze on the sofa in her living-room one afternoon. Mary sneaked over and held Martha's hand while she slept.

Mary then twitched her nose, just as she had seen Martha do. Her whiskers did not glow but she felt a slight tingle in her hand.

When she looked at her sleeping friend on the sofa, she noticed that Martha's whiskers had turned golden and were glowing! Mary was very excited and shouted:

"I'd love a chocolate fountain!"

… but of course, nothing happened.

(Why do you think it did not work? That's right because the spell did not begin with an 'M')

Then Mary remembered this rule and tried again:

This time she shouted:

"Make me a chocolate fountain!"

Suddenly, a big fountain appeared on the coffee table and lovely liquid chocolate was pouring out of it into a large bowl.

The chocolate kept changing from white to light brown to dark brown as lots of different flavours appeared.

It made a nice swirly pattern in the bowl.

Mary was delighted and started dipping things into the chocolate to see what they tasted like. She tried:

- Strawberries: yummy!
- Banana: nicer with the dark chocolate
- Apple: strange, but nice
- Grapes: little bombs of chocolatey juice
- Cheese: YUK!
- Toast: soggy

Soon Mary's tummy was full and she stopped dipping things into the chocolate …

… but the fountain did not stop.

The bowl kept filling up with chocolate and was soon full and overflowing onto Martha's nice carpet!

"Stop the fountain!"

… she shouted, but it kept on flowing. Mary did not know what to do next so she thought she should wake Martha up.

By the time Martha was fully awake, Mary was standing in a pool of chocolate above her ankles; she could not see her feet at all. Martha was shocked to see the mess.

"Mary, what had you been up to?" she yelled.

"Oh, just a little magic" said Mary, looking sheepish, "I have tried stopping the fountain but it doesn't seem to work".

"You have to say the spell backwards to stop it. What, EXACTLY, did you say to make the fountain appear?"

"I can't remember. It might have been 'I want a chocolate fountain'".

"That would not work. It doesn't begin with 'M'", said Martha.

"Oh, yes. Silly me, I keep forgetting that", said Mary.

Mary tried had to remember what spell she had used.

"Maybe it was 'Magic me a fountain' … so try 'Fountain a me magic', Martha", she cried, now standing up to her knees in chocolate.

"I can't try it. You have to do it. You made the spell", shouted Martha getting more worried as the chocolate crept up the side of the sofa she was on.

Mary gave it a go …

"Fountain a me magic!"

… she shouted, but the river of chocolate kept on flowing.

"THINK, MARY. What did you say?" said Martha.

(Can you remember what spell Mary used to make the fountain appear?)

By this time Mary was up to her waist in chocolate. Martha grabbed Mary's hand and pulled her up onto the sofa beside her.

"It might have been 'Make me a fountain'", said Mary.

"Fountain a me make!"

… she tried, but it still did not work.

By this time the sofa was floating on a sea of chocolate and they were heading up to the ceiling as it got deeper and deeper.

"You might have said, 'Make me a chocolate fountain'", suggested Martha, "Try that backwards".

"Fountain chocolate a me make!"

… Mary shouted as her head hit the ceiling. Suddenly, the fountain disappeared and the chocolate sea stopped rising.

"PHEW!" sighed Mary, "That was close."

"Look at the mess of my living-room", said Martha, "I'll have to use magic to clear it all up".

"But not yet!" said Mary.

She produced two straws, one for each of them.

"You can magic all this mess away after we've drunk some of the yummy chocolate sea".

Chapter 23

Costume Crossover

It was going to be a very busy day for the two mousey friends.

Mary's music group were playing a concert at the Albert Hall and Martha's gymnastics team were doing a tumbling display at the Olympic Park. They were both very excited as they packed their little rucksacks with their costumes and some snacks for lunch. Mary also had a little box with her flute in it. She was pleased to be playing the flute today so that she did not have to carry her cello on the bus.

They had agreed to meet at the bus-stop and would travel together to the middle of London and then split up and take the underground train (the 'tube') to their separate events. They waited on two different platforms at the tube station and could see each other across the tracks.

"Bye Mary, have a good concert. I'm sorry I can't be there to hear it", shouted Martha who was travelling east.

"You too, Martha. I'm sure the gymnastics display will be great. Take care, though; don't break any bones!" Mary shouted back from the west-bound platform.

Their two trains arrived at the same time and they waved to each other as the doors closed.

When Mary arrived at the Royal Albert Hall, the other members of the orchestra were getting ready. They had all been told to wear smart black clothes. Dinner Jackets (DJs) for the men and long black dresses for the ladies. Everyone was busy getting changed into their smart gear so Mary opened up her rucksack.

Except it wasn't HER rucksack! Inside, instead on the nice black dress which she had chosen that morning, was a bright pink leotard. It was

Martha's gymnastics bag; they must have swapped their rucksacks by mistake when they got off of the bus!

Mary suddenly wished that she was to be playing her cello, at least she could have hidden behind it on the stage. There was nothing she could do; she had to play her flute with a pink leotard on while all the rest of the orchestra were dressed in black!

Then she had a good idea. She remembered that the music they were playing was called 'The Magic Flute' so she strode onto the stage waving her flute about like a magic wand.

The audience clapped and cheered thinking this was all part of the performance.

That was lucky!

It was such a success that the conductor told everyone in the orchestra that they could wear whatever they wanted for the second part of the concert. They were playing 'Music for the Royal Fireworks' so the audience just thought that the bright coloured tee-shirts and shorts that they had on were like a fireworks display!

Now for poor Martha!

At the other side of London, she was about to get changed for her gymnastics display. She opened 'her' rucksack and found Mary's long black dress. Martha realised that she must have taken Mary's bag by mistake. Some people in the changing room had already seen the black dress so it was too late to use her magic to change it; she would have to wear it.

But she did not have to wear ALL of it. It was too long to do tumbles in so she got a pair of scissors and cut the dress above her knees. But, it was still black and everyone else was wearing bright colours.

Martha had a good idea. She took some flowers from the vases which were decorating the room they were in. She stuck the flowers through the lacy bits on Mary's dress to make a spectacular outfit.

The gymnastics display went ahead as planned and it was a great success.

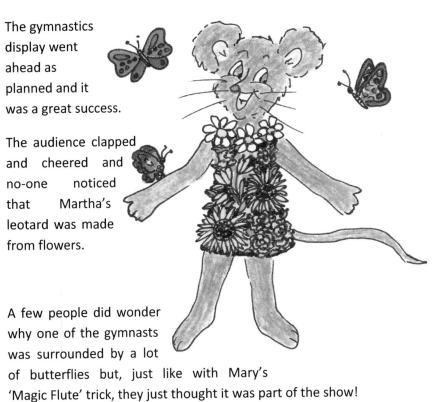

The audience clapped and cheered and no-one noticed that Martha's leotard was made from flowers.

A few people did wonder why one of the gymnasts was surrounded by a lot of butterflies but, just like with Mary's 'Magic Flute' trick, they just thought it was part of the show!

Chapter 24

Fashion Show

Martha and Mary were organising a Fashion Show at the local library. Lots of their mousey friends offered to help. Each person had to make up a costume out of things they found at home.

Some used bits of old sheets or pillow-cases from their beds. Others cut up old curtains to make dresses. One mouse even had a lamp-shade on her head like a big hat *(she said she felt a bit 'light-headed').*

Each of the friends would walk along a raised platform in front of the audience, showing off their costumes. In other fashion shows, this platform is called a 'catwalk' but Mary and Martha called theirs a 'mousewalk'.

(Why do you think they called it that?)

Mary and Martha were going to be the judges and they would decide which costume was the best. The winner would get a bag of Martha's home-made perkin biscuits and a jar of Mary's home-made jam.

The audience were all sitting in chairs very close to the mousewalk so they could get a good look at the different costumes.

'Pete, the cheat' had sneaked into the library through an open window before the doors were opened to let people in. He managed to grab a seat in the very front row.

Everyone else took their seats and the fashion show began.

"First of all we have Monica Mouse", said the announcer with a microphone, **"Her outfit is called 'Kitchen Creation'"**. Monica was wearing a colander on her head. She had two soup ladles for ear-rings and forks and spoons hanging from a belt around her waist. She jangled a lot as she walked down the mousewalk. Everyone clapped and cheered really loudly. They had to make a lot of noise or they would not have been heard over the din Monica was making.

"Next we have Morris Mouse whose outfit is called "Superhero Selection", said the announcer.

Morris had:

- A Spiderman mask
- A cape with the Batman logo
- Captain America's shield in one hand
- Thor's hammer in the other hand
- Superman's logo on his chest

He looked a bit strange, but no stranger than Monica's 'Kitchen Creation' before him.

At least it would be good to have a superhero there in case anyone caused trouble …

(which was very likely with Peter around).

'Pete, the cheat' was sitting on a chair with his feet up on the 'mousewalk' and he was trying to trip up the models as they walked along showing off their costumes.

Martha was angry and told him to get his feet off of there … "AT ONCE".

Peter grudgingly took his feet down and muttered a complaint:

"Mutter, mutter, mutter", he said grumpily and opened up his rucksack.

"Our third fashion designer today is Melissa Mouse. Her design is called 'Space Monster School Uniform'", said the announcer.

(What do you think a Space Monster wears to school?)

Peter was now eating a large picnic which he had taken out of his rucksack. He was chomping on apples and crisps and slurping juice from a can. He was making so much noise that the others could not hear the announcer.

While everyone was marvelling at Melissa's mysterious outfit, Mary crawled on her hands and knees to where Peter was sitting. He was too busy scoffing his picnic to notice her. She carefully untied each of his shoe laces and tied them both together.

Now his left shoe was attached to his right shoe. Mary crept back to her seat beside Martha before anyone noticed that she was gone.

By this time the announcer was getting fed-up with Peter's rude noises and told him to be quiet.

"If you don't stop eating, you'll be put out of the library", he said.

"Oh no, I won't", said Peter.

"Oh yes, you will!" said everyone else.

"GET-OUT-OF-IT!" they shouted.

When Peter stood up and tried to walk, he tripped over because his shoe-laces were tied together.

He fell flat on his face and the ice-cream cone he had been eating stuck to his nose.

The announcer said, **"That serves you right for being such a pest all day"**.

Peter struggled to his feet, pulled off his shoes so that he could walk and ran for the door in his socks. One of his socks said 'Wednesday' on it and the other said 'Monday'. Someone shouted:

"But today is Saturday!" and lots of people laughed.

Martha felt a bit sorry for Peter and, although she thought that he needed to learn how to behave himself, she wanted to help him.

Martha quickly made herself magical while everyone was laughing and then she said:

"Modify his socks!

Make them both Saturday socks!"

Peter's socks both changed to have the word 'Saturday' on them but, unfortunately, they were 'last' Saturday's socks. They had been lying in his dirty washing basket for a whole week without being washed. They were very stinky!

Peter ran out of the library door before anyone could smell his feet!

The fashion show continued without any more interruptions and the prize for the best costume was awarded to Melissa Mouse for her space monster outfit.

(By the way, you were right about what you thought a Space Monster would wear to school.

Maybe you could draw a picture of it to show everyone!)

Chapter 25

Gallery Robbery

Martha and Mary had gone to visit a big art gallery in London. They wandered about looking at all the paintings. Most were of people and places but some were a bit strange. There were pictures of bowls of fruit and flowers and one just had squares of different colours on it!

"I quite like the flowers", said Martha, "But I don't understand the one with the coloured squares".

"Me neither", said Mary, "It's weird, and the one with the fruit is making me hungry".

The two mice had been in the gallery for a long time so they decided they'd better use the toilet before getting the bus home. While they were washing their hands, the lights all went out!

"What's going on?" they shouted.

When they left the toilet, they found that the whole gallery was in near darkness; there were only a few emergency lights on. They ran to the front door and found that it was locked. The staff had all gone home and locked up the gallery while the two mice were still inside.

They could not get out!

Now, Martha could have used her magic to get them out but she remembered that her Granny had said not to use it too often.

Anyway, she thought it would be quite exciting to spend the night in the gallery.

They could have another look at all the paintings.

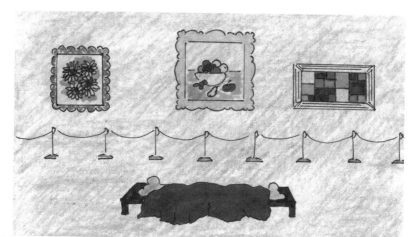

After another quick look, they found a bench with soft cushions on it and snuggled down for the night.

It was quite cold so they took a large curtain from one of the windows to keep themselves cosy.

In the middle of the night, Mary suddenly heard a noise.

"Wake up, Martha!" she whispered "There's someone here".

Martha woke up and they could both see someone moving around inside the gallery with a torch. It was a robber who had broken in through a window to steal some paintings.

Martha told Mary to sit up on her shoulders and then she covered them both with the curtain that they had been using as a blanket. They looked like a ten-foot high ghost!

Mary made herself magical and said:

"Make us float in the air!"

The double-decker mouse-ghost floated around the corner in front of the robber. His eyes grew wide with fear when he saw them and he ran back to the window where he had come in, shouting "Help, Mummy!"

He jumped back out of the window, right in front of a policeman who happened to be passing the gallery. The robber was captured and taken away in a police-car.

Another policeman came in to fix the broken window and saw Mary and Martha. They had stopped floating by this time and had taken off the ghost-curtain.

"What are you two doing in here at night?" he asked "Are you robbers too?"

The two friends tried to explain that they had bought tickets to visit the museum and that they had been locked in by mistake. The policeman did not believe them. He took them to the police-station and locked them up!

Don't worry, though.

The next day, they all went back to the gallery and spoke to the young man at the front desk. He had a name-badge which said:

'ROBERT JAMIESON – HERE TO HELP'.

Robert was indeed very helpful.

He said that he remembered Mary and Martha buying tickets for the museum the day before; they were not robbers.

(Clever Robert, he really saved the day!)

Then ...

- The policeman said "sorry" for not believing them.
- The gallery manager said "sorry" for locking the doors without checking that no-one was in the toilet.
- Mary and Martha said "sorry" for pulling down one of the curtains.
- The robber said "sorry" for trying to steal the paintings.
- Robert Jamieson was made 'employee of the week' for resolving the problem.

Chapter 26

Three Craws

One day, Mary decided that she had not played her tuba for a long time and would like to have a practice.

(Do you remember where Mary keeps her tuba? ... That's right, in her garden shed because it's too big to fit into her house)

She took the tuba out of her shed and sat on a bench in the garden with it in front of her but, when she blew into it, nothing happened!

No sound; nothing!

She could not understand what was going on; this had not happened before. She stood on the bench and looked inside the big trumpety end of the tuba and ... *guess what she saw?*

There was a bird's nest inside her tuba! A bird must have managed to get into her shed and decided that the big, hollow instrument was the perfect place to build its nest.

Mary carefully took the nest out of the tuba and lay it down on her garden wall.

She saw that there were three eggs inside it.

At that moment, the mummy bird flew into the garden; it was a big, black crow.

"Where are my babies?" she cried, "What have you done with my eggs?"

"Your eggs are fine", said Mary, "I had to move them so I can play my tuba. Your nest is here on top of the wall; perfectly safe".

"My eggs are about to hatch and I have no food for my babies", said the frantic crow.

"Don't worry", said Mary, "I'll look after them while you go and collect some food for your family".

"Oh, thank you", said the crow and flew off to look for worms and caterpillars.

As soon as the crow left, one of the eggs cracked open and a little baby crow crawled out. It fell out of the nest, right off of the wall and landed in Mary's foot. It was too small to fly yet.

"AYAH", said Mary and the bird at the same time.

Mary quickly put the little bird back in the nest, just as the second egg hatched. This little bird did exactly the same: right out of the nest and BOINK off of the wall. This one was not so lucky and landed on a brick and hurt its jaw.

"AYAH", it shouted even louder.

Mary picked it up and put it back in the nest with its brother. Then the third egg hatched. This bird did not even try to fly; it just started crying:

"I want my Mummy!" it wailed.

"Your Mummy had just gone to get you some dinner", explained Mary but the three baby crows were not happy. Mary tried to sooth them by playing a tune on her tuba but the birds just kept on crying. The louder Mary played, the louder the birds cried.

"WAAAAAAAA!" they all cried.

At this point Martha appeared and wondered what all the noise was about with three birds wailing and a tuba blasting out a tune.

Martha remembered a song her Scottish Granny used to sing to her when she was little. It was called 'Three Craws' (Craws is the Scottish word for Crows). She started to sing the song and Mary played along with her tuba. The song told the story of the three craws sitting on a wall on a 'cold and frosty morning'.

When Martha sang 'Mor-ning", Mary played two loud 'PARPs' on her tuba.

"On a cold and frosty PARP-PARP", the two friends played.

(You should find out more about this song!)

Soon the three crows/craws in the nest fell asleep and the garden became nice and quiet again.

The mummy bird arrived back with some food and was delighted to see that her three babies were out of their eggs and were all sound asleep in the nest.

They looked so cosy and comfy.

The mummy craw said that she was worried that a cat might see the nest on top of the wall and that she'd have to start building a new one in a bush were it would be hidden.

Martha told her not to worry and made herself magical. She cast a spell:

"Mrs Crow needs a new nest!"

A lovely new nest with four separate sleeping areas appeared in the bush at the bottom of the garden. It was high enough to be out-of-reach of passing cats.

Mary and Martha carefully lifted the sleeping baby birds into their new beds.

What a surprise they would get when they woke up.

They would have a new bedroom each ...

... and a yummy dinner!

Chapter 27

Camping Trip

One day, during the Easter holidays, Mary said to Martha:

"Wouldn't it be nice to see Trevor and Declan again? I really enjoyed meeting them in Edinburgh".

"Yes", replied Martha, "We did say that we'd like to see more of Scotland. Let me phone Cousin Trevor and see if they are free".

Trevor suggested a trip to the isle of Arran, off the west coast of Scotland.

The mice took the train up from London to Glasgow and then they all planned to take the ferry from Ardrossan to Brodick on the island.

Trevor had wanted to fly in his helicopter but Declan said:

"It would be nicer if we all took the boat across to Arran together".

"Do you remember the last time we were in a boat?" said Trevor, "The engine broke down and you had to use your ears as a propeller".

"Don't worry, Trevor", said Declan, "this is a huge ferry which takes cars and everything, not just a wee rowing boat".

So, they all met up at Glasgow Central Station and travelled together to the ferry port. When they got on the ferry, they went to the lounge to find a seat for the short crossing.

"I hope nobody gets sea-sick" said Martha, looking at Declan and Trevor.

The two rabbits tried to pretend that they were OK but Martha noticed that they did not have anything to eat during the crossing and were looking a bit ill when they arrived on the island.

The four friends had decided to camp out in tents for an adventure. They unpacked their rucksacks and set up their tents in a field overlooking the sea.

Mary and Martha went for a walk along the beach and the two rabbits decided they would play a trick on them. They put plastic spiders inside the tent where the mice were to be sleeping, thinking that they would be scared. When they came back from the beach, Mary and Martha went straight into their tent and came out with the pretend spiders in their hands.

"Good try, boys", said Mary "but these don't scare us".

Trevor and Declan said they would go and look for some wood to start a fire to cook their dinner on.

While they were away, Martha magicked up a campfire in the space in front of the two tents. She said:

"Make me a blazing fire!"

... and a little pile of burning wood appeared.

When Trevor and Declan arrived back with the wood, they were amazed.

"That was quick!" Declan said, "How did you manage to start a fire already?"

"Oh, just magic!" said Martha for a joke, winking at Mary.

Declan cooked the dinner and the four all ate burgers and potatoes which had been baked in the fire. Mary then brought out a guitar and played some songs which they all sang together.

When it was time for bed, Trevor and Declan got into their tent and said "Good night" to the two mice who were heading for their own tent.

When Trevor took off his shoes, the smell from his stinky left foot was so bad that Declan made him put them outside the tent. Yes, he made Trevor put his shoes AND his stinky foot outside. Trevor had to sleep with his left foot sticking out under the tent door.

They all fell fast asleep … well, Declan and Trevor did!

Trevor was making LOUD snoring noises which kept Mary and Martha awake. They could hear him from the next tent.

Declan slept like a baby because he had taken his ten ears off to make a nice soft pillow. He could not hear a thing!

The two mice sneaked over to the rabbits' tent. They had to put pegs on their noses to avoid the stink from Trevor's shoe and foot. Once inside the tent, Martha quickly took the peg from her nose and pinned it onto Trevor's nose.

He immediately stopped snoring, but he could not breathe anymore.

His face started to go very red!

Redder and redder he got until he let out a huge "PAH" and started to breathe through his mouth. Trevor did not even wake up!

He still made a bit of a noise but nothing like the racket he had been making before.

The mice went back to their own tent, yawning. They were very tired after their long journey up from London, but before they went to sleep they plotted some tricks they would play on the rabbits to get them back for the plastic spiders.

"We could let down the ropes on their tent and let it fall on their heads", suggested Martha, "or we could put salt in their tea at breakfast time".

"We'll think of something", said Mary as she drifted off, dreaming of what adventures they would all get up to the next day.

(I wonder what will happen. Do you?)

Chapter 28

Goatfell

Next morning, when the four friends woke up, they discovered that it had been raining overnight. Trevor's shoes and his left foot were soaking wet because they had been outside the tent all night. When he went to put his shoes on, there was a huge frog in one of them.

(Guess which one? Yes, the right one. Even a frog would not go near Trevor's left shoe; it's far too stinky).

The rain overnight had put out Martha's fire. She was about to magic up another one when she saw that Trevor and Declan were watching her.

"Oh dear", she thought, "I nearly forgot. They still don't know about my magic so I can't use any spells".

Without a fire, they could not cook bacon and sausages so they all just had cold cereal for their breakfast. They had brought Snap, Crackle and Pop with them in their rucksacks and a very kind cow in the next field said that they could have some of her milk.

Their plan was to climb a hill called Goatfell today. Martha asked why it was called that and Declan said it was because a goat fell down the hill a long time ago.

"It fell from the top of the hill and bumped all the way to the bottom; making huge holes in the ground as it went", he said. Mary thought this was the funniest thing she had ever heard and she laughed and laughed. Martha was not so sure that Declan was telling the truth; she thought he was just making it up to impress Mary.

As they set off to climb the hill, Trevor's feet were making a 'squelch, squelch' noise as he walked. His shoes were still soaking wet but at least he had remembered to remove the frog before putting them on!

It was a long, slow climb up the hill and every time they passed a hole in the ground, Declan said:

"Look, that's where the goat fell."

Mary would burst into a fit of giggles and the other two just looked at each other with raised eyebrows and silently shook their heads. They could not see why Mary found Declan's jokes so funny.

Goatfell was a very high hill (the highest on Arran) but they struggled up to the very top. The views were magnificent and all four were glad they had managed to climb all the way.

On the way back down, they found it very hard not to run. But they had to be careful because if anyone did start to run they would find it very difficult to stop.

At one point, Mary tripped and started to run down the hill. She could not stop herself. Faster and faster she went until her little mouse legs were about to give up. Trevor was walking beside Martha. Declan was ahead, a bit further down the hill.

"I need to save Mary", said Martha and twitched her nose to make herself magical. Her whiskers started to glow golden, much to Trevor's surprise (remember, he did not know that his cousin could make magic).

She was just about to cast a spell to help her friend when Declan turned around and saw Mary careering down the hill towards him at great speed. He stuck his arms out and caught Mary as she sped past.

"Oh, thank you, thank you, Declan; my hero", said Mary.

"No problem, Mary. Have a wee rest here" said Declan and they waited for Trevor and Martha to join them.

"Well done, Declan. You really saved the day again", said Trevor. He was remembering another time Declan had used his ears as a propeller on a boat. He saved the day then too.

Mary was still out of breath and a bit shaky so they all sat down on a rock beside the path.

"Let's all have a drink of water to refresh ourselves", said Martha as she handed water bottles to everyone (winking at Mary as she did so).

Martha secretly made herself magical and whispered:

"Make springy snakes!"

When Trevor opened his bottle to have a drink, a huge snake jumped out and gave the two rabbits a fright. It was not a REAL snake, but a plastic one on a spring, like a jack-in-the-box. Still, Trevor and Declan got such a fright that their ears all stood straight up in the air!

Mary and Martha giggled.

When Declan opened his bottle the same thing happened. Once again a springy snake leapt out.

This time their ears, which were already standing up on top of their heads, fell right off. Their thirteen ears all landed in the little stream which was running down the hill behind them.

Mary and Martha giggled even more.

Trevor and Declan ran down the hill chasing after their ears which looked like little boats in the stream. Eventually, the stream flowed into small loch and the rabbits' ears floated out into the middle where they could not be reached.

"Oh no! What are we going to do?" said Trevor, but Declan could not hear him as he had no ears on.

"Oh no! What are we going to do?" repeated Declan.

(How are they going to get their ears back? Find out next time)

Chapter 29

Magic Revealed

Trevor and Declan were stomping about on the little beach beside the loch. Their ears were still floating on the water; out of reach. The two rabbits had to use hand signals and lip-reading to talk to each other as they could not hear anything.

Mary and Martha were still sitting on the rock up the hill having a nice drink of water.

"That serves them right for trying to scare us with plastic spiders yesterday", said Mary.

"Yes, but I suppose I'd better help them now", replied Martha.

She made herself magical and shouted:

"Miggly Meagle!"

Martha turned into a big golden eagle and flew down the hillside and over the loch. She picked up all of the ears with her huge claws and flew back to the beach with them.

Declan and Trevor were amazed!

The rabbits thanked the mysterious bird who had just rescued their ears, not knowing that it was really Martha, although Trevor did notice something strange about it.

By the time they had sorted out their ears between them, Martha had changed back into a mouse and she and Mary had joined them on the beach.

"Well, that's been quite an exciting walk today", said Mary, "I think we should head back to our campsite now.

The four friends walked wearily down the rest of Goatfell; Mary and Declan in front and Martha and Trevor a little bit behind them.

When the other two were far enough ahead that they could not hear him, Trevor asked Martha about what he had seen; how her whiskers had started to glow when she tried to save Mary. Then he added:

"I also noticed that the golden eagle who rescued our ears from the loch had a little yellow ribbon around its neck, just like you have. What's going on, Martha?"

Martha decided it was time to tell her cousin about her magic.

"Granny Lucy says I should only tell 'good friends' and I suppose you are my good friend, Trevor", she explained, "Mary already knows and I think Declan is a good friend too".

When they got back to the camp-site, they were all very tired and their legs were sore from all the walking they had done.

Martha decided to tell Declan about her magic.

"I can't believe you're magical. Show me", he cried, excitedly. Martha twitched her nose and said:

"Maybe a hot bubble-bath would be nice!"

A big tub of hot bubbly water appeared; just like the ones you get at swimming pools. The four friends jumped in and the hot water made their sore legs feel better.

Later, when the hot tub had disappeared, Martha magicked up some dinner for them all. She got them all to hold hands and said:

"My friends' favourite meals, please!"

Four plates of food appeared. Each of the friends had their favourite:

- Spaghetti Bolognese for Declan
- Fish Fingers and Beans for Mary
- Chicken and Gravy for Trevor
- Mince and peas for Martha

They all had some dried mango for pudding.

After they had finished their dinner, the clouds parted and there was a full moon in the clear, black sky.

Martha said: "Do you know what is REALLY magical?"

"No, what?" the others asked.

"Being able to share a great time on this wonderful island with good friends", she replied.

"Even if we <u>do</u> play tricks on each other", added Mary.

Chapter 30

'Hoppy' Birthday

Mary was having a special birthday and there was to be a huge party in Camberwell library for her.

Mary had spent the night in Martha's spare bedroom so that the two mice could get ready together in the morning.

Martha decided to wear the same hat as she had worn to the Royal Garden Party.

"My Scottish Granny would be proud that I'm getting good use out of it", she told Mary.

Mary didn't care that Martha was wearing the same hat as before. She was the birthday girl and would be wearing a new spotty dress and a new green ribbon. She felt very special.

Trevor and Declan had come down from Edinburgh and had shared a room at a hotel in Peckham, just along the road. The hotel had a yellow three-wheeled car outside, just like the one on the TV programme they liked to watch.

The rabbits were also up early to get themselves ready for the party. They checked that their ears were clean (no potatoes growing behind them) and that they were all stuck on properly. There would be Scottish dancing in the library and they did not want any of their thirteen ears falling off as they jigged about.

They put on their nice clean kilts; Trevor's was a blue tartan (his favourite colour) and Declan's was red (his favourite colour).

All of their friends from London and Edinburgh were going to be there. Even Peter had promised to behave and, in return, Mary had said he could come to the party.

Their friend Dig-Down 'D', the mole, had tunnelled all the way from Scotland. He said he had stopped off in Garforth, near Leeds, for a sandwich and glass of milk before continuing his long journey south. He had a copy of the London Tube Map with him so that he would not bang into any of the underground train tunnels by mistake.

Dig Down 'D' had brought a birthday present for Mary. It was wrapped up in pink and white striped paper tied up with a pink ribbon.

Granny Lucy was there too and she had made a special cake. She had heard about the chocolate fountain incident and so she had made a chocolate cake.

There was lots of food (cheese and apples and perkins, of course) and milk, juice and water to drink … as well as the yummy cake.

Even 'Pete, the cheat' was enjoying himself and behaving himself too. He had put on his favourite red jumper especially for the party.

When it was time to start the dancing, everyone looked at Mary and wondered if she would play the music.

Mary said she would be delighted to play for all of her friends but that she really wanted to dance at her own birthday party.

She couldn't do both!

... or could she?

Martha had a 'good idea'.

She and Mary went out into the corridor of the library and Martha made herself magical. As soon as her whiskers were glowing, she shouted:

"Multiply Mary!"

Suddenly, there were six more Marys in the corridor, each with a different musical instrument. Everyone clapped and cheered when the 'Mary Dance Band' appeared and started to play great Scottish Country Dance tunes.

Mary got to dance AND play the music.

The Dancing Rabbit Chorus from Portobello sang a few of their favourite songs and danced along. Trevor and Declan are members of this choir so they joined in too.

Mrs O'Hare was conducting the singing and she was soon exhausted from waving her arms about.

After a while, Mrs O'Hare was glad to join Granny Lucy at a little table at the side of the dance-floor where they drank cups of tea and watched the 'young ones' dancing.

"This has certainly been a Happy Birthday for dear Mary", said Granny Lucy.

"With all these dancing rabbits, it's more like a 'Hoppy' Birthday", said Mrs O'Hare and they both laughed.

See if you can find all these things in the picture:

- Trevor
- Declan
- Mrs O'Hare
- Dig Down 'D'
- The Chocolate Cake
- Martha's Hat
- 7 Marys
- Pete, the Cheat

After the party, Mrs O'Hare said that she was not looking forward to the long journey back to Portobello. Granny Lucy said:

"If you can keep a secret, I'll show you a quick way home".

"That would be great. I can't wait to get home to my flat and get into my own bed", said Mrs O'Hare.

Granny Lucy told her about the magic door marked 'Library Link'. They both went through it and found themselves back in Corstorphine Library in Edinburgh.

"This is great!" cried Mrs O'Hare, "I'll jump on a number 26 bus and be back home in half-an-hour".

Back in Camberwell, the party was a great success.

Martha, Mary, Trevor, Declan and all their friends were having a great time.

More Bedtime Stories

The Rabbit with Three Ears

Trevor and Declan first appeared in my other book of bedtime stories, called *'The Rabbit with Three Ears'*.

It is available in various formats:

- Paperback - ISBN 978-1-722-34263-6
- Kindle from Amazon
- ePUB from Lulu Bookstore
- Apple iBook from iBookstore

Trevor, the Rabbit with Three Ears, gets up to tricks with other rabbits, pigeons, a seagull, a fox, a dog, a mole and a cat.

GJ Abercrombie

38886511R00074

Printed in Poland
by Amazon Fulfillment
Poland Sp. z o.o., Wrocław